CONTENTS

Don't miss a single one of Spork's adventures!

ALIEN IN
THE OUTFIELD

by Lori Haskins Houran
illustrated by Jessica Warrick

KANE PRESS
New York

Spork

Trixie Lopez

Mrs. Buckle

Jack Donnelly

Grace Hanford

Piper Cho

Adam Novak

Newton Miller

Jo Jo

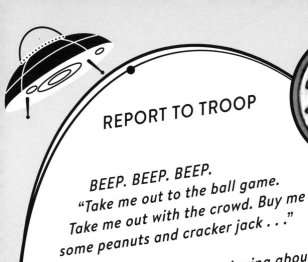

REPORT TO TROOP

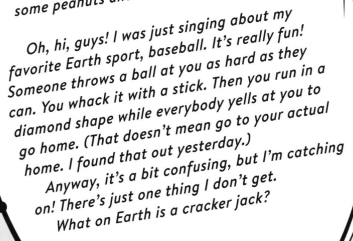

BEEP. BEEP. BEEP.
"Take me out to the ball game.
Take me out with the crowd. Buy me
some peanuts and cracker jack . . ."

Oh, hi, guys! I was just singing about my
favorite Earth sport, baseball. It's really fun!
Someone throws a ball at you as hard as they
can. You whack it with a stick. Then you run in a
diamond shape while everybody yells at you to
go home. (That doesn't mean go to your actual
home. I found that out yesterday.)
Anyway, it's a bit confusing, but I'm catching
on! There's just one thing I don't get.
What on Earth is a cracker jack?

1

NIFTY FIFTY

"I call Adam's team!" said Trixie.

"No fair!" said Jack. "You got to be on his team yesterday."

"Let's do Rock, Paper, Scissors," Grace suggested.

"Is that like Dust, Meteor, Lasers?" asked Spork. "That's how we decide things on my planet."

Adam smiled at the little alien.

"Guys, recess isn't for another hour,"

he said. "We can pick teams then."

Adam loved that the class was so into baseball. When he first suggested playing a couple of weeks ago, nobody seemed that excited. But now they were hooked. They wanted to play every recess!

He loved that they all wanted to be on his team, too. They said he was the best player in the class. Secretly, Adam agreed. Jack was a good pitcher and Trixie ran the bases super fast. But nobody could hit like him.

Adam swung a pretend bat.

CRACK! The ball soars over the left field wall . . . and the crowd goes wild!

"Okay, everybody. Get out your maps!" called Mrs. Buckle.

Ugh, thought Adam. His pretend home run turned into a foul ball.

Mrs. Buckle was teaching the third grade about the fifty states. For two weeks, they'd been singing state songs, playing state games, and doing state puzzles. They even ate a State Plate lunch, with food from around the country! (Adam liked the Texas chili best.)

Most of it was fun, but there was one part Adam couldn't stand—map time. Every morning Mrs. Buckle gave them a list of states and a blank map of the country. They were supposed to fill in the states . . . all *fifty* of them!

Grace could already do it. So could Newton. Their photos were on the Nifty Fifty wall at the front of the room. Their smiling faces beamed down at Adam.

How was he ever going to get on that wall? No matter how hard he tried, he couldn't remember where the states belonged. He could swear they switched places when he wasn't looking!

He bent over his map and chewed his pencil. *Think, Adam,* he told himself.

The state that poked out at the top might be Maine. Florida was the droopy one down in the corner . . . wasn't it? And the really big state was Texas. Or maybe Tennessee.

What about the states in the middle? Two of them looked exactly the same—like plain old rectangles! How was anybody supposed to remember *those*? He started to write *Colorado* in one rectangle. Then he crossed it out and wrote *Nebraska.* Then he crossed *that* out and put in *Utah.*

"Done!" Jack shouted.

"Seriously?" said Adam.

"Of course," said Jack, holding up his finished map. "It's easy."

Easy?

Adam looked at his own paper. It was mostly scribbles.

Mrs. Buckle came over to check Jack's map. "Great job!" she said. "Let's get your photo for the wall!"

Jack made a big cheesy grin while Mrs. Buckle took his picture.

Adam glanced over at Spork's desk beside him. Some of the spaces on Spork's map were empty, but at least a dozen were neatly filled in.

Great. Even Spork knows more states

than me, thought Adam. *And he's not from this country. Or this PLANET!*

Adam crumpled up his map and shoved it into his desk.

"I give up," he muttered. He put his head down and waited for the recess bell.

He needed to hit a ball for *real*.

2

HOME SWEET HOME

"Wow! Nice hit, Adam!" said Newton.

"Thanks," Adam said. He felt better now. Smacking a triple could do that.

Spork came up to the plate holding a bat in his orange hands.

"Come on, Spork," Adam called from third base. "Hit me home!"

Jack threw a pitch. *WHOOSH!* The ball whizzed past Spork.

"Strike one!" hollered Jack.

Another pitch. Another *WHOOSH*.

"Strike two!"

On the third pitch, Spork swung so hard he spun around in a circle. His baseball cap went flying.

"Strike three!" Jack yelled. "You're out! O-U-T *out!*"

"Knock it off, Jack," Adam said.

"What?" said Jack.

Adam called time out. He jogged to the pitcher's mound so he could talk to Jack in private.

"Spork's just learning to play," Adam said quietly. "Give him a break."

"I *did* give him a break!" Jack said.

"Those pitches I threw him were easy."

"Easy?" said Adam. He was getting sick of Jack saying that word. "EASY? Spork never even *heard* of baseball until two weeks ago. Hitting a ball isn't EASY for him!"

Jack rolled his eyes. "Whatever. I just hope he's never on my team."

"You don't have to worry about

that, because he'll be on *my* team," said Adam. "And you *won't*!"

The two boys glared at each other.

"Fine," Jack muttered, turning away.

Adam jogged over and picked up Spork's cap.

"Thanks, Adam!" said Spork.

Adam looked at Spork. The alien had been around for a while now, ever since his spaceship crashed on the playground back in September. But Adam hadn't spent much time with him yet.

"Hey, Spork," he said. "Want me to help you out with your hitting?"

Spork's eyes lit up. "Really?"

"Sure. I could stay after school and give you some tips."

"COSMIC!" yelped Spork.

Adam figured that meant *yes*.

That afternoon, Adam pitched—
and pitched and pitched—to Spork.
"Here comes another one," he said.
"Remember, keep your eye on the ball."

Spork swung. "Oof!" Then his
shoulders slumped. "That's seventy-
eight misses in a row."

"Don't worry." Adam went over
and patted Spork on the back. "My big

brother threw me about a thousand pitches before I got the hang of it."

"I miss yubble." Spork sighed.

"Yubble? What's that?" Adam asked.

"A sport on my planet. I'm pretty good at it. Almost as good as you are at baseball!"

It was Adam's turn to sigh. "I might be good at baseball, but I'm not good at anything else," he grumbled.

"Hi, boys."

Adam turned around. Mrs. Buckle was standing right behind him, holding a tote bag stuffed with books.

"Greetings, Mrs. Buckle!" Spork said. "Adam's been teaching me to hit!"

"Yes, I saw that," said Mrs. Buckle. "I could tell you were trying really hard." She looked Adam in the eye. "I know you've *both* been trying hard lately."

"What are *you* doing?" asked Spork.

"Just heading home for the night," said Mrs. Buckle.

"Home?" Spork looked confused. "Don't you live here?"

Mrs. Buckle gave a little chuckle. "Sometimes it feels that way! But I do

have a house of my own. See you in the morning, guys."

"Bye!" said Spork.

Adam waved to Mrs. Buckle. Then he picked up his ball and bat. "I guess I'd better go, too."

"Of course," said Spork. "We have homework—studying the states!"

"Right," Adam said, frowning. "Hey, let's practice your hitting every day after school, okay? If you keep trying, I know you'll get the hang of it."

"Okay! Thanks!" said Spork.

The whole way home, Adam felt like a game of catch was going on in his brain. First he'd think about baseball and helping Spork. That made him feel good. Then he'd think about maps and states. That made him feel bad.

Good, bad. Good, bad. Back and forth, back and forth.

Adam shook his head. *Forget about the map stuff,* he told himself. He was useless at it anyway.

He was going to think about nothing but baseball until bedtime!

3

READY, SET, YUBBLE

All night Adam dreamed of grand slams and cheering fans.

But when he got to school the next morning, his stomach hurt.

Mrs. Buckle will pass out the maps again, and I won't do any better than yesterday, he thought. *I'll probably do WORSE!*

Mrs. Buckle surprised him, though. "We're going to do something different today," she said.

She leaned against the front of her desk. "I know you've all been learning a lot of new things, inside *and* outside the classroom. That takes perseverance."

"Purse-and-*what*?" said Trixie.

"Perseverance," Mrs. Buckle said again. "It means sticking with something until you get it. Not giving up."

Adam shifted in his seat. He had said "I give up" just yesterday, right before he crumpled his map.

"Today I'd like to learn something new along with you," said Mrs. Buckle. "That is, if Spork will take over teaching for a bit."

"Who, me?" said Spork.

Mrs. Buckle smiled. "Yes, Spork. I heard you mention a game yesterday—I think it was called yubble? Would you teach us how to play?"

Spork jumped up so fast his chair tipped over. "Of course!" he cried. "You're going to love it. Yubble is a great game!" Then his forehead crinkled. "There's just one problem. We don't have any vorbets."

"What's a vorbet?" asked Newton.

"It's a special kind of ball on my planet," Spork explained. "Vorbets are super light and sort of floaty. This might sound strange, but we use our mouths to puff them full of air."

"Wait, do you mean *balloons*?" Trixie said.

"There's a whole bunch of balloons in the front office!" said Grace. "They had them for Principal Hale's birthday."

She ran out and came back with her arms full.

"*VORBETS!*" said Spork. He tapped a

	Balloon	Vorbet
✔	Superlight	✔ Superlight
✔	Floaty	✔ Floaty
	Smells like feet	✔ Smells like feet

small blue balloon in the air. "They're not regulation size, but they'll do. Can we take them outside, Mrs. Buckle?"

"Lead the way!" Mrs. Buckle said.

Everyone followed Spork to a patch of ground beside the school. Adam helped him draw a big rectangle in the dirt with a stick. Then they drew an X to connect the opposite corners.

"This is the yubble court," Spork said. "We divide into four teams—"

"FOUR?" said Jack. "What kind of sport has four teams?"

"Let's listen, please," Mrs. Buckle said.

"The teams line up at the corners," Spork went on. "One player from each team taps a vorbet to the opposite corner and back. If the vorbet touches the ground it's called a groodle, and the player has to go back ten steps. Once a player makes it back to their corner, they pass the vorbet to the next person on the team. The first team to finish wins."

"Sounds easy," Jack said.

"Oh, I almost forgot!" said Spork.

"You can't use your hands. Only your knees and elbows."

"*What?* This is going to be crazy," cried Trixie. Then she grinned. "Crazy *awesome*!"

The class split into teams. Trixie, Adam, Mrs. Buckle, and Newton were the first four players. They each took a balloon.

"Hang on," Adam said, looking across at Trixie in the opposite corner. "How do we keep from crashing into the person coming the other way?"

Spork smiled. "That's half the fun," he said. "Ready . . . set . . . *YUBBLE*!"

4

TRY, TRY AGAIN

Tap, tap, tap!

Adam started across the court, tapping a balloon with his left elbow. It was harder than he expected! The balloon squirted away. He started to reach out to grab it.

"No hands!" Spork reminded him.

Adam lifted his knee instead and bopped the balloon back up to his elbow.

Tap, tap, tap!

Just when he was getting the hang of it, he saw Trixie heading right for him with her own balloon.

"Eek!" cried Trixie. "I'll go over, you go under!"

Trixie hit her balloon over Adam's head. Adam crouched down and dipped under Trixie's arm, bouncing his balloon on his elbow the whole time.

"*Knognackle!*" shouted Spork. "That's what we yell when someone does something great in yubble. It means *hooray*—times a hundred!"

Out of the corner of his eye, Adam saw Newton and Mrs. Buckle collide. Their balloons fell to the ground.

"Oops! Sorry, Newton!" said Mrs. Buckle.

"We groodled!" Newton said, grinning.

"That's okay! Just take ten steps back and try again!" Spork called.

By the time Adam passed his balloon off to Grace, sweat was trickling down his back.

Grace started tapping. "This is hard," she said, "especially since I can't stop laughing!"

Adam looked around. It was pretty funny. Kids were jerking their elbows in the air, like a bunch of chickens flapping their wings! Balloons were bouncing all over the place. The class was having a blast . . . except for Jack.

"This is dumb," Jack said, dropping his balloon for the third time. "I quit!"

"You can do it, Jack," said Spork. "Just keep your eye on the vorbet."

Newton and Mrs. Buckle finally made it back to their home corners. Newton tapped the balloon to Piper, who took her turn and passed it along to Spork. "Here you go!"

Spork was off!

He raced across the court, tapping the balloon smoothly from elbow to elbow.

When he got to the opposite corner, Spork didn't stop to turn around. Instead he did a backflip with a twist!

While he was upside-down, he gave the vorbet a quick tap with his knee.

"Did you see that?" said Grace.

"Whoa!" cried Adam.

Spork's team cheered when he got back to his corner. "We won!" Newton said.

"Who cares?" said Jack, kicking his balloon. "This game is impossible. It's only easy for Spork because it's an alien game, and he's an alien!"

"Is that true, Spork?" Mrs. Buckle asked, panting a bit. "Is yubble easy for you?"

"Oh, no, it's very tricky," said Spork. "You should have seen me when I first started playing. I groodled all the time! I had to practice for *eons* to get this good."

"Interesting," said Mrs. Buckle. "Why don't we take a break in the shade before we head inside?"

The class spread out under a big oak tree. Mrs. Buckle flopped down on the grass with them.

"*Phew!* I had fun playing yubble," she said. "But that's not the only reason I wanted to do it today. I wanted to show you that learning new things is a challenge for *everyone*—including me.

It took me four tries to get across the yubble court!"

She stopped to wipe her forehead. "There's an old saying: *If at first you don't succeed, try, try again.* Next time you tackle something new, be patient with yourself. Take a deep breath. And remember—try, try again."

Adam turned the idea over in his mind. It was really the same thing he had told Spork about hitting. You have to keep trying, even if it takes a thousand pitches.

The class headed inside. Mrs. Buckle announced free time until lunch, but Adam went straight to his desk. He found his map and smoothed it out.

"I can do this," he said. "Try, try again."

As soon as he started, he felt his head spin.

Why do there have to be fifty states? he thought. *Why can't there be, like, fifteen? No—five!*

Then it hit him. What if there WERE only five states . . . at least for today?

Adam ran up to Mrs. Buckle's desk. "Five! Five states!"

"What do you mean, Adam?" Mrs. Buckle said.

"Can I just study five states today?" Adam asked. "That doesn't seem so hard. And if I do the same thing for ten days, I'll know all fifty of them!"

"YES!" Mrs. Buckle said. "I *love* that idea! I know you can do it, too."

"You do?" said Adam.

Mrs. Buckle put her hand on his shoulder. "Anyone who can clobber a baseball like you knows a thing or two about perseverance. Go, Adam, go!"

5

KNOGNACKLE!

Adam stuck with his plan.

Every morning, he picked five states to study. Every afternoon, he pictured them in his head while he pitched baseballs to Spork. And every night, he wrote them on a map right before he went to sleep.

Meanwhile, he watched the Nifty

Fifty wall fill up with faces. Trixie.
Shani. Kyle. Spork.

"Pretty crowded up there, isn't it?"
said Jack.

Adam didn't answer. He knew what
Jack was getting at—that Adam was the
only kid in the whole class who hadn't
made it onto the wall.

It's okay, he told himself. *Just keep
going.*

He was close. He knew forty-five
states now. Forty-five! If he could learn
the last five states tonight, his picture
would be on the wall *tomorrow*!

"I still mess up the ones in the
middle," he told Spork on the way to
recess. "Those two rectangle states drive
me crazy!"

"Really? They're my favorites," said Spork. "They're shaped like yubble courts! I always remember the top one is Wyoming because it has a y in it, for yubble—the top sport in the galaxy!"

"Oh, yeah! That's neat!" said Adam. "How do you remember the other one?"

"That's Colorado," said Spork. Then he whispered, "*Rado* is kind of a rude word on my planet. Sometimes people say it

when they groodle. Not me of course!"

Adam laughed. But Spork's face turned serious.

"Adam, you've learned almost all of the states, but I still haven't hit the ball," he said. "Not once!"

"You will," said Adam. "Don't give up!"

"Guys, are you coming?" Trixie yelled. "We're starting!"

Spork and Adam hurried the rest of the way to the field. Jack was already on the pitcher's mound. Trixie stepped up to the plate.

SMACK! She hit the ball hard and ran to first.

"Good one," said Grace, the first baseman.

"Thanks!" said Trixie.

Spork was up next. Jack smirked.

"Easy out!" he said under his breath.

Adam gritted his teeth. *I wish Spork would bash the ball over the fence right now. That would show Jack!*

"You've got this, Spork," Adam called. "You can do it. Just like we practiced!"

Jack threw a pitch.

Spork swung.

Tink!

The bat hit the ball . . . just barely! The ball plopped at Spork's feet. It dribbled a little ways toward the pitcher's mound, then stopped.

"Run!" yelled Adam.

Trixie was already sprinting for second, but Spork hadn't moved.

"That counts?" said Spork.

"YES! *RUN!*" Adam yelled again.

Spork raced toward first base. Jack rushed to scoop up the ball and throw it to Grace, but he was too late.

"*Safe!*" said Adam. "Spork, you did it! You got a hit!"

"I did it! I did it!" Spork cried, jumping up and down.

"Big deal. It was a measly bunt, not a home run," scoffed Jack.

"It is a big deal," said Trixie. "Spork had purse-a-whatever!"

"Perseverance," Grace said.

"Exactly!" Trixie put her hands on her hips. "He didn't *quit*—unlike some people I know!"

Jack's face turned bright red.

"Great job, buddy," Adam told Spork. He felt like a proud coach. Spork had kept trying, just like Mrs. Buckle said, and it had paid off.

I hope my purse-a-whatever works, too, he thought.

Tomorrow he'd find out.

Mrs. Buckle laid a fresh map on Adam's desk first thing the next morning.

"Ready?" she asked.

Gulp! Adam nodded.

He started writing. Five states. Ten states. Fifteen. Twenty!

He was down to the middle states when he felt a pinch of panic.

The rectangles! I can never remember the two rectangles!

He took a deep breath to calm himself down. Then he broke into a grin.

"Oh, yes I can!" he said out loud.

Y for yubble, the top sport in the galaxy.

He wrote *Wyoming* in the top rectangle.

Rado is a bad word on Spork's planet. . . .
He put *Colorado* in the bottom rectangle,
giggling a little when he wrote the last
four letters. Then he gave the paper to
Mrs. Buckle.

Adam chewed his pencil while he
watched his teacher put little checkmarks
next to each state.

Please, please, please, please, please . . .

"Perfect!" Mrs. Buckle declared. "Adam,
you did it! Congratulations!" She ran to
her desk to grab her camera.

Everyone clapped while Mrs. Buckle
took Adam's picture—the last picture for
the wall! Even Jack joined in.

"It's almost recess. Let's celebrate with a
game of baseball!" Trixie said.

Jack cleared his throat. "Um, I have

another idea." He pulled a package of balloons out of his desk. "How about a game of *yubble*?"

Everyone stared. Spork's mouth fell open.

"What? I've been practicing," said Jack. Then he blushed. "I didn't want to be a quitter. You guys didn't quit, and that's . . . well . . ." Jack paused. "That's pretty cool," he admitted.

Spork gave Jack a high-five. After a second, Adam did, too.

"I'm proud of you, Jack," said Mrs. Buckle. "And Adam. And *all* of you!" She looked up at the Nifty Fifty wall. "There's so much to cheer about, that only one word will do. *Hognuckle!* No, wait. *Fognickle!* Oh, my. Help me out, Spork!"

"*Knognackle!*" cried Spork. "*KNOGNACKLE*, everybody!"

REPORT TO TROOP

BEEP. BEEP. BEEP.
Hi, *munch* guys! Guess what? I *munch munch* found out what a cracker jack is. It's the yummiest *munch* snack in the universe! I'm sending you a *munch munch* whole box of it!
Well, maybe not a WHOLE box . . .
Munch munch munch.

ACTIVITIES

Greetings!
In the Galaxy Scouts we say, "Don't stop until you reach the farthest star." That means don't give up! Earthlings call this per . . . per . . . perseverance. (Even saying the word takes some work!) Try this quiz, don't give up, and you'll soon be a Persevering Pro!
—Spork

(There can be more than one right answer.)

1. Whenever you try to dance the Martian Mambo, it's like you have two left feet. (And you're not even from planet Sinstra!) How do you deal?
   a. Ask a friend to mambo with you every day after school. Practice makes perfect.
   b. Take up extreme crater climbing instead.
   c. Tell everyone you're too good to dance with them. You only dance with the stars.
   d. Make up your own moves. Maybe the Funky Spacejunk will catch on!

2. Your friend keeps crashing his spaceship into meteors. How can he persevere?
   a. Ask you to drive his spaceship for him.
   b. Sign up for a class at the Galactic Driving Center.
   c. Park his spaceship and only take the Big Bang Bus.
   d. Slow down and practice in familiar orbits before driving his ship on the interplanetary highway.

3. You're having a hard time learning the names of the moons. You:

   a. Ask a Lunar Guide for extra help.

   b. Study a few moons every night until you know them all.

   c. Yell "Rado!" and give up.

   d. Make up a silly tune to remember their names.

4. You keep hitting vorbets too hard and bopping them out of bounds. You:

   a. Only play on the yubble court surrounded by a fence. That way the vorbet can't go out of bounds.

   b. Bop the vorbet twenty times in a row, each time with less force.

   c. Set a goal to bop fewer vorbets out of bounds in each game you play.

   d. Hit that vorbet as hard as you can. Who cares where it goes!

Answers:

1. When you try something new, it takes time to get good. Don't quit, so cross out b. You probably won't make many friends with c, and while d is an inspired idea, you'll never get better at the Martian Mambo that way. Practice is always a good way to improve, so a is a great answer.

2. You might want to help your friend by driving his ship for him, but that doesn't help him persevere, so steer clear of a. Same with c. B is a great answer because he can get lessons on how to improve. And d is good because he can practice in safer areas until he's a better meteor-dodger.

3. When things get tough, don't give up, so cross off c. Answers a, b, and d are all good ways you can work on learning the moons.

4. Cross out d because hitting the vorbet harder would not help. You know practicing and setting goals are good things to do, so both b and c are excellent options. A fence would keep the vorbet in, but it doesn't help you persevere or improve, so don't choose a.

Shaken-Up Signs

We are planning a school-wide yubble tournament. We all have jobs to do to get ready. Newton and Grace made a sign for the field. My job is to hang it up.

I was so excited to get to the field this morning that I ran the whole way here. But when I opened my bag I realized I had shaken up the letters. I don't want to mess this up. Please help me unscramble each of the words so that I can hang the sign before my friends get here!

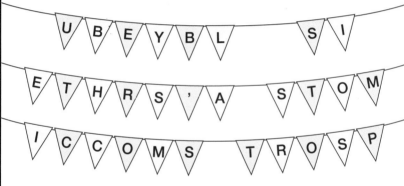

Answer: YUBBLE IS EARTH'S MOST COSMIC SPORT. (Funny coincidence: In my language, STOM ICCOMS TROSP means "Let's go play!")

Spork's Space Jokes

Q. Why did the sun go to school?
A. To get brighter!

MEET THE AUTHOR AND ILLUSTRATOR

LORI HASKINS HOURAN has written more than twenty books for kids (not counting the ones her flarg ate). She lives in Florida with two silly aliens who claim to be her sons.

JESSICA WARRICK has illustrated lots of picture books about dogs, cats, and kids, but she is mostly interested in drawing aliens, for some strange reason. She does a pretty good job acting like an Earthling . . . most of the time.

Spork just landed on Earth, and look, he already has lots of fans!

★ **Moonbeam Children's Book Awards Gold Medal**
Best Book Series—Chapter Books

★ **Moonbeam Children's Book Awards Silver Medal**
Juvenile Fiction—Early Reader/Chapter Books
for book #1 *Spork Out of Orbit*

"Young readers are going to love this series! Spork is a funny and unexpected main character. Kids will love his antics and sweet disposition. Teachers and parents will appreciate the subtle messages embedded in the stories. The kids in the stories genuinely like each other, which I found refreshing. I will be giving these books to my young friends."—**Ron Roy**, author of A to Z Mysteries, Calendar Mysteries, and Capital Mysteries

"A breezy, humorous lesson in honesty that never stoops to didacticism. The other three volumes publishing simultaneously address similarly weighty lessons—lying, shyness, bullying, and responsibility—all with a multicultural cast of Everykids. . . . A good choice for those new to chapters."
—**Kirkus** for book #1 *Spork Out of Orbit*

"This is a book where readers, kids, and aliens learn together, experiencing how words and choices affect all of us. It's simple, elegant, and very insightful storytelling. *Greetings, Sharkling!* doesn't waste a single page of opportunity."
—**The San Francisco Book Review**

"I'm so glad Spork landed on Earth! His misadventures are playful and sweet, and I love the clever wordplay!"
—**Becca Zerkin**, former children's book reviewer for the *New York Times Book Review* and *School Library Journal*

"Kids will love reading about Spork. Parents, teachers, and librarians will love reading aloud this series to those same kids."—**Rob Reid**, author of *Silly Books to Read Aloud*

How to Be an Earthling
Winner of the Moonbeam Gold Medal
for Best Chapter Book Series!

Respect

Honesty

Responsibility

Courage

Kindness

Perseverance

Citizenship

Self-Control

To learn more about Spork, go to kanepress.com

Check out these other series from Kane Press

Animal Antics A to Z®
(Grades PreK–2 • Ages 3–8)
Winner of two *Learning* Magazine Teachers' Choice Awards
"A great product for any class learning about letters!"
—*Teachers' Choice Award reviewer comment*

Let's Read Together®
(Grades PreK–3 • Ages 4–8)
"Storylines are silly and inventive, and recall Dr. Seuss's *Cat in the Hat*
for the building of rhythm and rhyming words."—*School Library Journal*

Holidays & Heroes
(Grades 1–4 • Ages 6–10)
"Commemorates the influential figures behind important American
celebrations. This volume emphasizes the importance of lofty ambitions
and fortitude in the face of adversity…"—*Booklist* (for *Let's Celebrate Martin
Luther King Jr. Day*)

Math Matters®
(Grades K–3 • Ages 5–8)
Winner of a *Learning* Magazine Teachers' Choice Award
"These cheerfully illustrated titles offer primary-grade
children practice in math as well as reading."—*Booklist*

The Milo & Jazz Mysteries®
(Grades 2–5 • Ages 7–11)
"Gets it just right."—*Booklist,* starred review (for *The Case
of the Stinky Socks*); *Book Links'* Best New Books for the Classroom

Mouse Math®
(Grades PreK & up • Ages 4 & up)
"The Mouse Math series is a great way to integrate math and literacy into
your early childhood curriculum. My students thoroughly enjoyed these
books."—*Teaching Children Mathematics*

Science Solves It!®
(Grades K–3 • Ages 5–8)
"The Science Solves It! series is a wonderful tool for
the elementary teacher who wants to integrate reading
and science."—*National Science Teachers Association*

Social Studies Connects®
(Grades K–3 • Ages 5–8)
"This series is very strongly recommended…."—*Children's Bookwatch*
"Well done!"—*School Library Journal*

KANEPRESS.com